Adapted by Ellie O' Ryan

Based on the series created by Dan Povenmire and Jeff "Swampy" Marsh

Based on the Disney Original Movie, "Phineas and Ferb: Across the 2nd Dimension"

Written by Dan Povenmire, Jeff "Swampy" Marsh, and Jon Colton Barry

DISNEP PRESS

New York

Published by Disney Press, an imprint of Disney Book Group.

No part of this book may be reproduced or transmitted in any form
or by any means, electronic or mechanical, including photocopying,
recording, or by any information storage and retrieval system, without written
permission from the publisher. For information address Disney Press,
114 Fifth Avenue, New York, New York 10011-5690.

Printed in the United States of America

First Edition

1 3 5 7 9 10 8 6 4 2

J689-1817-1-11121

ISBN 978-1-4231-4262-1

For more Disney Press fun, visit www.disneybooks.com

Visit DisneyChannel.com

CHAPTER 1

The moment Phineas Flynn woke up, he could tell it was going to be a great day. First, it was yet another day of summer vacation. Second, there wasn't a cloud in the sky. Third—and most importantly—Phineas already knew that he and his brother, Ferb Fletcher, were going to do something amazing. Now all they had to do was figure out what!

Just then, the boys' pet platypus, Perry, crawled onto Phineas's pillow and started chattering.

"Good morning, Perry," Phineas said. "Now *that's*

the way to wake up. This is gonna be the best day ever!"

Ferb looked at Phineas and nodded. He was ready to have some fun, too.

The two boys scrambled out of bed and quickly got dressed. Then they slid down the banister into the living room.

"Good morning, boys," their dad, Lawrence Fletcher, said.

"Happy anniversary, Perry!" Linda Flynn-Fletcher, their mom, said at the same time.

"Oh, that's *right*!" Phineas exclaimed. "Gosh, I can't believe that it's been five years. I remember the day we first got you!"

A big grin crossed Phineas's face at the memory of walking into the Danville Animal Shelter when he and Ferb were just little boys.

"Come on, kids!" their dad had encouraged them. "Pick out any pet you want!"

"Oh, look, Phineas," their mom said. "This one's looking at you!"

"And *this* one's looking at you, Ferb," their dad added, pointing to an animal in a cage.

"Why won't anything look at *me*?" whined the boys' older sister, Candace Flynn.

Then Phineas noticed something. "Ferb, this one is looking at *both* of us at the *same time!*"

The boys peered into a cage that held a very strange-looking animal. It had a thick tail, an orange beak, two paws, and two flippers! Nobody in the family could tell exactly what it was.

"*That* thing?" Candace asked, making a face. "You're kidding, right?"

Phineas and Ferb looked at each other and nodded. They both agreed that this was the perfect pet for them!

"Is there something I can do for you?" asked an employee as she approached them.

"We'd like that one, please," Mr. Fletcher said.

"You'd like to adopt the *platypus*?" the employee asked in surprise.

"Oh, is that what it is?" Mr. Fletcher asked brightly.

"Well, yes. May we have him, please?"

"Okay," the employee said with a shrug.

"What would you even *name* a platypus?" Candace asked.

"Bartholomew!" Phineas suggested.

"Bartholomew!" echoed Ferb.

But the platypus wasn't quite so enthusiastic about that name. He made a strange sound in response.

In the living room, Phineas snapped back to reality and leaned down to pet Perry. "And then when we got you home, we renamed you Perry . . . and got you this locket," he recalled. Phineas opened it to reveal photos of Phineas, Ferb, and their pet. "Look how young we all were!"

But there was one person in the Flynn-Fletcher house who wasn't paying any attention to the talk about Perry's anniversary. Upstairs, Candace was psyching herself up for a very important phone call to a very cute guy—her crush, Jeremy Johnson. She dialed his number and held her breath until he answered.

"Hey, Jeremy, want to go to the mall today?"

Candace asked, hoping she sounded a lot cooler and calmer than she felt.

"You know, I'd love to," Jeremy said on the other end of the phone. Candace started to do a victory dance around her room.

"But my dad's taking me to check out his old college today," Jeremy finished.

Candace stopped dancing. In the background, she could hear Jeremy's dad yell out, "Hoo-yah! Go Polecats! Hoo-yah!"

"Gee, Jeremy, I forgot you were a whole year older than me," she said. "A trip to college, heh, heh. That's really great. Okay, well, I'll talk to you later. Bye."

Candace hung up the phone and sank down onto her bed. She picked up her teddy bear, which had a picture of Jeremy's face taped onto its head, and gave it a sad hug. But something more serious than Jeremy not being able to join her at the mall was bothering her.

"Jeremy, in the blink of an eye, you'll be moving

on to the next phase of your life," Candace said to her teddy bear. "You'll be going to college and wearing tweed jackets with patches on the elbows. You'll be so mature. And look at me! I'm a *child*!"

Candace stood up with a determined glint in her eyes. "Jeremy, you'll see," she vowed. "I can be *mature*. Starting with taking this silly photo off!" She ripped Jeremy's picture off the teddy bear and blinked in surprise. "Oh, Mr. Miggins, have you been there the whole time?"

In the backyard, Phineas, Ferb, and Perry were playing one of their favorite games: *platy*pult baseball! As Ferb placed a baseball on Perry's outstretched tail, Phineas stepped forward with a bat. But Phineas was more than just a player. He was also the announcer!

"All right, looks like the pitcher's ready and . . . batter up! Batta-batta-batta swing!" Phineas shouted as he swung the bat.

Crack! The baseball soared across the yard.

"Oh, yes, sports fans, that may be the best hit ever in the history of platypult baseball!" Phineas cheered. "And the crowd exhales loudly through their mouths! And Fletcher snags the pop fly . . . he's out!"

"Hi, Phineas!" their friend, Isabella Garcia-Shapiro, called out as she strolled into the backyard. "Whatcha doin'?"

"Turning Perry's involuntary reflex into a sporting event," Phineas explained.

"Hi, Perry," Isabella said with a wave. "Can I try?" She grabbed the bat, swung, and hit the ball over the fence.

"Whoa, mama!" Phineas exclaimed. "Nice shot, Isabella!"

Then their friends Baljeet Rai and Buford Van Stomm arrived. "Did someone lose a ball?" Baljeet asked, carrying it in his hands.

"Yeah, we were just playing platypult baseball," Phineas replied.

"Oh, I *love* platypus-themed sports!" Baljeet cheered.

"You know, if we had *two* Perrys, we could put a net between them and play platypult badminton," Phineas realized. "Ferb, that's it! *I* know what we're gonna do today!"

Everyone knew that when Phineas had an idea, something amazing—something exciting—something unbelievable was about to happen! The kids got right to work on building Phineas's latest idea: two giant platypults, so they could play platypult badminton!

"Okay, everyone," Phineas announced a little later. "I think the tail is all set. I'll just go check with the foreman."

Phineas glanced around, but he didn't see Perry anywhere.

"He's gone," Isabella realized.

"Hey, where's Perry?" Phineas asked with a frown. "Did he *really* slip away? On his *anniversary*? Sometimes it seems like Perry has missed every single cool thing we've done all summer long!" He shrugged his shoulders. "I guess he can do whatever he wants. After all, it's his day, right?"

"Hey, what was that small noise?" Baljeet suddenly asked.

"Let's all go walk over to it," Phineas suggested.

What the gang didn't know was that Perry was hiding in the backyard and had thrown a pebble across the yard to distract them. And there was something else they didn't know: behind his cover as a friendly pet, Perry was actually a secret agent! From his code name (Agent P) to his fedora, this fearless platypus had dedicated his life to fighting evil in all of its forms—most especially in the form of Dr. Doofenshmirtz, whose sinister plots put the entire Tri-State Area in danger.

With the group distracted, Agent P made his move, zipping across the yard into a secret entrance to his underground lair. He landed on his chair as the large view screen crackled to life. An image of Major Monogram, the commander of the agency that Perry worked for, suddenly appeared onscreen.

"Ah, good morning, Agent P," Major Monogram's voice boomed. "Quick word: recently, you've been having some close calls. Your host family has almost caught you sneaking into your lair several times. No need to remind you that if your cover is blown, you'll have to be transferred to another city with another host family. And we both know you wouldn't like that. Ha, I remember the day you were first assigned!"

Major Monogram smiled as he remembered his assistant Carl Karl's first time going undercover— as the animal-shelter employee who gave Perry to Phineas and Ferb!

"Agent P, as you know, every operative is equipped with an autoscan replication device, just like the one in your hat," Major Monogram continued. "We've been using the information you've gathered to replicate every one of Dr. Doofenshmirtz's–inators. Our top men have been analyzing them to determine if they've been getting smarter or dumber. And, to be honest, the jury's still out. Now, we find out that he's building an alternate-dimension-related-inator. Anyhoo, your assignment is to stop him before

he finishes building it! Behind you, rising dramatically from the floor, is Carl with some high-tech gadgets you might find useful."

Agent P spun around to see a platform rising from the floor—but it was empty.

"Uh, sir?" Carl's voice piped up from below. "I didn't step on it in time. Would you mind lowering the platform again?"

"That's really killed the moment," Major Monogram replied as he pressed a button.

When the platform rose again, Carl was standing in the middle of it, surrounded by an impressive array of contraptions.

"*Voilà*, monsieur!" Carl cried. "This first item is our new wrist communicationizer. It has many applications that will help you in the field. For example, it has a powerful directional electromagnet. It will draw any metal object to you!"

Carl activated the watch, and his glasses flew off his face and stuck to the magnet. "See? And these are *aluminum*!" he bragged.

"Quit goofing around, Carl, and show him the hologram," Major Monogram barked. He crossed his arms and tried to remain calm.

"Yes, sir," Carl replied as he pressed another button on the watch. Suddenly, a hologram of Major Monogram beamed out of it.

"Heh! Pretty nifty, huh?" the hologram of Agent P's superior officer chuckled. "With this device, you'll be able to contact me from anywhere at any time . . . but don't call between three-thirty and four, 'cause that's when I take a shower. Wait—wait—whoa—whoa—wait a minute! Is that *me*?"

"Oh, no!" Carl shrieked. "His holographic projection has become mesmerized by his video image! I'd better shut it off." Carl rapidly pushed a button, and the hologram vanished. "And if you push *this* button, it gives your adversary an incredible ice-cream headache—"

Suddenly, Carl grabbed his head in pain. "Agh! Agh! Agh!" he cried. "You better watch where you point that," he warned Agent P.

The platypus rolled his eyes, wishing that Carl would hurry up and finish the demonstration. Major Monogram hadn't exactly said so, but Agent P could read between the lines: if the agency felt the need to equip him with all this new high-tech gear, the threat from Dr. Doofenshmirtz must be very serious indeed.

And in that case, Agent P knew that there wasn't a moment to lose!

CHAPTER 2

Meanwhile, Candace's best friend, Stacy Hirano, had just arrived at the Flynn-Fletcher house. But what she saw in Candace's room shocked her. The place was a total disaster—even worse than usual—with stuff all over the floor and huge trash bags brimming with some of Candace's favorite belongings!

"Hey, girl! Uh, what are you doing?" Stacy asked, looking around.

"Stacy, Jeremy's going to college soon, and here I am concerned with busting my brothers to my 'mommy' and living in this nursery!" Candace announced, waving a ceramic unicorn in the air to make her point. "A unicorn, Stacy." She shook her head in disgust and threw the unicorn into a trash bag. "You've got to help me get rid of all this junk!"

Stacy's eyes widened. "Wow, bold move," she replied.

"Yep, good-bye, childhood folly. Hello, carefree, undemanding adult life," Candace said proudly.

From the hallway, Candace's mom started to laugh when she passed by her daughter's room and over-heard what Candace had just said. "Yeah, good luck with that," she said. "Candace, your father and I are off to the movies. You're in charge, okay?"

"Okay, Mom," Candace said as she ripped a heart-covered poster off the wall. After her mom was gone, Candace gave Stacy a serious look. "You know, I'm even thinking of giving up on busting my brothers," she told her.

"The irony is, that as a grown-up, you don't *need* to tell your mom," Stacy pointed out. "You can just bust them yourself."

Candace's whole face lit up. "That's *it*!" she exclaimed. "Stacy, I'm old enough to bust them myself!"

"That's what I just said," Stacy replied.

But Candace didn't hear her as she strode over to the window and stared into the backyard. She knew that the backyard was the main place where Phineas and Ferb did bust-worthy things. She was certain she would find some kind of crazy invention outside.

Sure enough, she was right. There they were—two giant platypus-shaped structures right in the yard! From the look of what was going on outside, it was only a matter of time before Candace could put her new-found busting powers to use!

Across town, on the top floor of Doofenshmirtz Evil, Incorporated, Dr. Doofenshmirtz couldn't wait to unveil his latest evil invention. "Now, Perry the Platypus, quake in terror as I punch a hole through to another dimension. Behold! The Other-Dimensionato—"

"Sir?" Norm, a giant robot who was one of the doctor's inventions, spoke up.

"What?" yelled Dr. Doofenshmirtz.

"I've finished setting up the buffet," Norm replied in his robotic voice.

"Oh, for crying out loud, Norm, I was in the zone!" Dr. Doofenshmirtz cried.

"I just thought you were playing with your doll," Norm said.

"It's not a *doll*, it's a stand-in!" Dr. Doofenshmirtz shouted. "Pretendy the Practice-*pus*! See? I wonder if Perry the Platypus practices with a fake me? It would be nice to know he cares enough."

Agent P cared all right—but not enough to practice with a giant Dr. Doofenshmirtz doll! But Agent P was still in the lair, listening to Carl's demonstration.

"Of course, you'll only need this if you're attacked by one of the royals or a member of Parliament, so it's okay to leave the safety on," Carl said as he held up a dangerous-looking device. "And here's your brand-new rocket car. Sweet, huh? Good luck, Agent P!"

The platypus didn't have a moment to waste. He jumped into the rocket car and gunned the engine.

"Uh, Carl, did you tell him the accelerator's a little touchy?" Major Monogram spoke up.

Whoooosh!

The rocket car blasted off, smashing right through the ceiling!

"I think he knows, sir," Carl replied, staring through the gaping hole overhead.

At the same time, Phineas was preparing to launch one of their life-size platypults. Buford had already brought the other platypult to the park earlier and was waiting for them there.

Phineas and Ferb settled into a giant shuttlecock and fastened their seat belts. "Three . . . two . . . one . . . service!" Phineas yelled.

Baljeet released the trigger, shooting his friends high into the sky—where their shuttlecock crashed into Agent P's rocket car! In all the commotion, Phineas and Ferb didn't notice that the rocket car was piloted by their very own pet. The shuttlecock veered way off course—just as Candace stormed outside to bust her brothers.

"Phineas and Ferb, you are so bust—oh, my gosh!" she cried, looking around in shock. "Where did it go?" The platypus-shaped inventions that she had spotted a few minutes earlier had vanished!

Candace ran up to Baljeet and Isabella and grabbed their shoulders. "You there! Small children! Where's the big contraption?"

"I don't know," Isabella said, looking around. "It was here just a moment ago!"

"It disappeared?" Candace gasped. "Stacy, do you realize what this means?"

"We're done?" Stacy asked.

"No!" Candace cried. "Some kind of mysterious force *always* takes away Phineas and Ferb's inventions before my mom shows up. This time it took away their invention before *I* showed up. The mysterious force recognizes that I am now a *grown-up*!"

"A mysterious *force*?" Stacy commented. "I'm not buying it."

"Well, I'm going to prove it to you, *and* bust my brothers at the same time!" Candace declared. She turned back to Baljeet and Isabella. "Where are my brothers?"

"We just launched them toward the park," Baljeet said helpfully. "Buford is there with the other platypult."

"Okay, as the adult, I decree that we are going to the park," Candace announced. "Does anyone need to go potty first?"

But Candace didn't realize that the crash had pushed the shuttlecock wildly off course. It wasn't headed for the park anymore.

Instead, it was headed toward the headquarters of Doofenshmirtz Evil, Incorporated!

Inside, Dr. Doofenshmirtz was fiddling with his newest –inator. "Hmm, needs a little something," he muttered.

"Ferb, it looks like we're going to hit the building that looks vaguely like your head," Phineas said, right before they smashed though the glass walls—and crashed onto the –inator, smashing it into pieces!

"All right, what's with the giant shuttlecock?" Dr. Doofenshmirtz shouted.

"We're really sorry, sir," Phineas said. "I don't know what happened. One minute we were innocently launching ourselves across the city in a badminton platypult, the next thing we know we're bouncing on up to the east side to your deluxe apartment in the sky."

"Well, it looks like you totaled my Other-Dimensionator," complained Dr. Doofenshmirtz.

"An Other-Dimensionator?" asked Phineas curiously. "What does it do?"

The evil doctor sighed. "Well, at the moment, it just stops giant shuttlecocks, apparently, but it's supposed to let me go into other dimensions," he reported.

"Oh, that's cool!" Phineas exclaimed. "We can help you fix it. I'm Phineas, and this is my brother, Ferb. And you are?"

"I'm Dr. Heinz Doofenshmirtz, but my friends call

me . . ." Dr. Doofenshmirtz's voice trailed off as he realized that he didn't *have* any friends. He sighed again. "I just got in such a funk."

"Ferb is naturally handy with tools. I bet we could put this thing back together in no time!" Phineas said excitedly.

"Ah, what the heck," Dr. Doofenshmirtz said with a shrug. "Before we start, there's a whole buffet set up here. Please partake. I was expecting someone who seems to be running late." He glanced toward the steel doors, wondering what could be keeping Agent P.

But Phineas and Ferb went right to work trying to fix the –inator. "Okay, field compressor attaches to the auxiliary generator. . . . Was this working before?" Phineas asked.

"Well, if by working you mean 'functioning properly,' then no," Dr. Doofenshmirtz admitted.

"I think I see your problem," Phineas said. "Everything's wired through this self-destruct button. Do you even need that?"

"Well, of course I need—wait a minute. No, I do *not* need that! You are absolutely right," Dr. Doofenshmirtz realized.

"So Ferb has rigged up this remote control so that if we get separated from the portal, we can open another one," Phineas continued.

"Nice touch, kid," Dr. Doofenshmirtz commented.

"I guess this is the last piece," Phineas said. "Ferb, boost me up."

"Ooh, I cannot wait!" cried Dr. Doofenshmirtz, clapping his hands.

At that moment, Agent P snuck into Dr. Doofenshmirtz's lair. But when he realized that Phineas and Ferb were there, he was horrified! He had no choice but to slip into his cover as Perry the Platypus—or risk permanent reassignment.

"Oh, *there* you are, Perry!" Phineas exclaimed as he spotted his pet.

"*Perry*?" repeated Dr. Doofenshmirtz.

"Yeah, he's our pet platypus," Phineas replied.

"Is *every* platypus named Perry?" the evil doctor

asked. He could hardly believe that his number one enemy shared a name with the boys' pet! What were the odds?

Phineas smiled. "In a perfect world, yes."

"Well, he's a cute little fella," Dr. Doofenshmirtz said, kneeling down to pet Perry. "Hi there, coochie, coochie—ouch! Ow! Ow!"

Perry bit down—hard—on Dr. Doofenshmirtz's finger. The doctor hopped around in pain, waving his hand in the air.

"Perry! *No!*" Phineas scolded him.

"Oh, it's okay," Dr. Doofenshmirtz said. "Platypuses don't typically like me."

"Well, Perry, you're just in time to see us open a portal to another dimension!" Phineas exclaimed.

Desperate to put a stop to this plan, Perry chomped down on a piece of the Other-Dimensionator and ran under the couch.

"Perry, no!" Phineas yelled again as he lunged for the part. "What are you doing? No, no! This is *not* tug-of-war! Silly boy."

Finally, Phineas wrestled the part away from Perry and gave it back to Dr. Doofenshmirtz.

"All right, let's get this show on the road, huh?" the evil doctor said.

"Okay, here we go," Phineas said as he positioned the piece back onto the Other-Dimensionator.

Agent P was desperate. That's the only reason why he did what he did next. He jumped on the couch, lifted his leg, and peed everywhere!

"Perry! No!" Phineas howled in horror. He couldn't believe what Perry had just done!

"What?" Dr. Doofenshmirtz asked. Then he noticed the stain on his couch.

"Not on the sofa!" groaned Phineas. "Oh, I'm sorry, Dr. D. We—we should take him outside."

"No, wait. It's all right," Dr. Doofenshmirtz said understandingly. "I was planning on replacing that old couch anyway. Let's light this pop stand, or however it goes. Aaaaaand *now!* Behold! The mind-blowing first images from beyond our dimensional reality!"

The machine immediately opened a shimmering

portal to another dimension. Phineas, Ferb, and Dr. Doofenshmirtz crowded around the portal excitedly, hardly daring to imagine what they might see on the other side.

But all they saw was furniture. "It's a couch," Dr. Doofenshmirtz realized. "Well, that's a bit anticlimactic, huh? I guess it's a nice couch, though. Hey, I've got an idea. Let's swap my couch for that one."

Phineas wasn't sure that was such a good idea. "Ummm . . ." he said slowly.

But Dr. Doofenshmirtz had already climbed through the portal! He grunted as he tried to pick up the couch. "I got it . . . I got it . . . maybe . . . uh . . . Come on, you want to give me a hand here?"

Phineas and Ferb, carrying Perry, hopped through the portal and looked around in awe. "Whoa! Awesome! Check it out!" Phineas exclaimed as he glanced outside. "Hey, Dr. D—look at this!"

Dr. Doofenshmirtz joined him at the portal. What he saw astonished him.

Everywhere he looked, Dr. Doofenshmirtz saw

enormous pictures of . . . himself! His face was plastered on every building and sign. All the bushes and trees had been sculpted in his image. The streets were full of Dr. Doofenshmirtz statues, and there were stores named after him!

"You're famous here!" Phineas marveled. He thought that was pretty cool.

Just then, a tram pulled up in front of the building. "Uhhhh, GET OFF!" a voice that sounded just like Dr. Doofenshmirtz's blared over the tram's speakers.

Dr. Doofenshmirtz took a closer look at one of the signs. "'Heinz Doofenshmirtz—your leader,'" he read. His eyes lit up. Could it really, *finally* be true?

Whatever strange dimension they had stumbled into, Dr. Doofenshmirtz never wanted to leave it!

CHAPTER 3

Behind them, someone cleared their throat. Dr. Doofenshmirtz spun around to see Major Monogram sitting at a concierge station.

But how could *that* be right? Major Monogram was a high-ranking officer in a top secret agency. He didn't work in reception. And he definitely didn't belong in an alternate dimension!

"Hello?" Dr. Doofenshmirtz asked in confusion as he walked toward the desk. "Aren't you—?"

"Is this some kind of a test?" the Major Monogram

look-alike asked nervously. "Is that really you, sir?"

Suddenly, it made sense. "Major Monogram's my slave in this dimension!" Dr. Doofenshmirtz exclaimed.

"I prefer the term 'indentured executive assistant,'" Major Monogram–2 mumbled.

"Well, I want to meet this other-dimension me!" Dr. Doofenshmirtz announced. "Where can I find him?"

"Oh, you're from another dimension," Major Monogram–2 said. "He'll probably want to see you then. . . . He's into that freaky sort of stuff. Have a seat, and I'll let him know you're on your way up."

Dr. Doofenshmirtz sat down in a fancy leather chair. "Oh, okay. So what, I just have to sit here and— *waaah*!" he suddenly cried.

As the chair zoomed down the hall on its own, Dr. Doofenshmirtz could only hold on tight—and scream! In moments, he arrived in the alternate Dr. Doofenshmirtz's chamber.

"That was awesome!" Dr. Doofenshmirtz shouted as the chair came to a stop.

Dr. Doofenshmirtz–2 looked at Dr. Doofenshmirtz with curiosity. "Do I know you?" he asked.

The two Dr. Doofenshmirtzes stared at each other. It was like looking in a mirror—an evil mirror, of course. The only difference between the two men was a sinister-looking patch over the alternate Dr. Doofenshmirtz's left eye.

"Yeah, I'm you from another dimension," Dr. Doofenshmirtz said casually.

"You're *me*?" Dr. Doofenshmirtz–2 asked in disbelief.

"Well, that would explain the handsomeness," Dr. Doofenshmirtz pointed out.

"Right back at'cha, big guy," Dr. Doofenshmirtz–2 said. "Does that mean you and I are exactly *alike*?"

"I suppose so," Dr. Doofenshmirtz replied.

The two Doofenshmirtzes realized that they had a lot of catching up to do. But there was one thing that Dr. Doofenshmirtz–2 couldn't quite understand. "So what you're telling me is you're *still* not the ruler of your Tri-State Area?" he asked in disbelief.

"Well, obviously, you did not have to deal with my nemesis, Perry the Platypus," Dr. Doofenshmirtz said defensively.

"Oh?" asked Dr. Doofenshmirtz-2. "Observe." He pressed a button to open a hidden chamber that contained a robotic platypus. "This is Perry the *Platyborg*! He was once my nemesis, but now he is the general of my army!"

"Wow, you're good!" Dr. Doofenshmirtz exclaimed.

"Dismissed," Dr. Doofenshmirtz-2 told the platyborg, as Phineas, Ferb, and Perry entered the room. "*Now* who's interrupting me? Remind me to berate my indentured executive assistant!"

"Oh, it's cool, man," Dr. Doofenshmirtz spoke up. "They're with me."

Dr. Doofenshmirtz-2 stared at Perry. An ugly scowl crossed his face. "You *dare* bring a secret agent in here?" he snarled.

"This boy's a secret agent?" Dr. Doofenshmirtz asked, pointing at Phineas.

"No, not *him*," snapped Dr. Doofenshmirtz-2.

"The quiet one?" Dr. Doofenshmirtz asked, pointing at Ferb.

"No, no, no, *him*!" Dr. Doofenshmirtz–2 shouted.

But Dr. Doofenshmirtz was still clueless. "This plant?"

"The *platypus*!" shrieked Dr. Doofenshmirtz–2. "That's secret agent Perry the Platypus!"

Phineas shook his head. "He's just a platypus. He doesn't do much," he said.

"Oh, this is rich," Dr. Doofenshmirtz–2 laughed. "I see what's going on. You—you really think that he's your pet, don't you? *Wrong!* He's *using* you. You're just his cover. He's a secret agent!"

When everybody looked at him as if he were completely crazy, Dr. Doofenshmirtz–2 realized that he hadn't yet convinced them.

"Here, let me prove it to you," he continued. "General Platyborg! Come down here at once!"

The platyborg appeared instantly and landed directly on his leader's foot.

"Ow!" Dr. Doofenshmirtz–2 yelled. "All right,

platyborg, you see that platypus? You know what to do."

The platyborg marched up to Perry—and punched him in the face!

"Perry!" Phineas screamed as he ran over to his pet. "What was that for?" he asked, staring at Perry the Platyborg. "Perry, are you okay? Ferb, how are his vitals?"

Dr. Doofenshmirtz–2's eyes narrowed. "Wait, let me try something," he said. "Oh, platyborg? Do the same thing to those two boys."

"What?" shouted Phineas and Dr. Doofenshmirtz at the same time.

The platyborg dutifully marched up to Phineas and Ferb, but before it could hit them, Agent P leaped into action—and knocked the platyborg clear across the room!

"*Perry*?" Phineas asked in amazement.

"*Yes*! I knew it!" Dr. Doofenshmirtz–2 cheered.

"Wait a minute, I'm confused," Dr. Doofenshmirtz said. "Why does their platypus fight so good?"

Agent P rolled his eyes at Dr. Doofenshmirtz's cluelessness as he put on his fedora.

"Perry the Platypus?" Dr. Doofenshmirtz gasped when he finally figured it out.

"Get them!" Dr. Doofenshmirtz-2 ordered his robot guards.

"You're a secret agent?" Phineas asked Agent P. "So *this* is where you disappear to every day? You come here and fight *this* guy?" he asked, pointing to Dr. Doofenshmirtz-2.

"No, he fights *me*," Dr. Doofenshmirtz argued. "He doesn't really know this guy."

"You fight a *pharmacist*?" Phineas asked Agent P. in confusion. "Why would you even *do* that?"

"Actually, I'm an evil *scientist*," Dr. Doofenshmirtz corrected him. "A lot of people are confused by the lab coat."

"You're *evil*?" Phineas asked incredulously. He turned to Agent P. "He's evil! So, not only have you been leading a double life this whole time, but you sat there and let us help an evil scientist open an evil portal into an evil dimension. And you did nothing to stop us!"

"Well, he did pee on the couch," Ferb spoke up.

"Wait a second!" Dr. Doofenshmirtz shouted. "I just realized—that was a conscious choice! You peed on my couch!"

"No, no, that wasn't enough," Phineas said, shaking his head at Perry. "*That's* when you should have put on your little hat. Not now, after we've gone through it, into this mess!"

"Oh, for badness sake, you can hash all this out in prison. Guards!" Dr. Doofenshmirtz–2 called out.

Agent P aimed his watch at Dr. Doofenshmirtz–2 and pressed a button. In seconds, the alternate evil doctor grabbed his forehead and fell to his knees. "Ow, brain freeze!" he hollered.

Agent P grabbed Phineas and Ferb and leaped out of the window. The brothers screamed in terror as they plunged in a free fall. But in the nick of time, Agent P's parachute opened, and they gently drifted down through the air.

"I'm sorry," Phineas said, looking at his pet. "I'm just having trouble processing this right now."

Agent P handed him a pamphlet. Phineas read the title out loud. "'So You've Discovered Your Pet Is a Secret Agent—'" He thrust the pamphlet back at Agent P. "I don't want your pamphlet!"

At that moment, the platyborg jumped out of the portal to follow them!

"Uh-oh. He's coming back around!" Phineas warned Agent P. A struggle began as the platyborg landed on them in midair. Suddenly, Agent P's legs got tangled in the parachute! He struggled to get free. Luckily, he was able to quickly untangle himself, and he, Phineas, and Ferb landed on a rooftop. Phineas and Ferb wrestled the parachute over the platyborg, causing it to plummet toward the ground.

Phineas let out a sigh of relief. That had been close! He turned to Perry again. "All this time, we're like, 'He's a platypus, he doesn't do much,'" Phineas complained. "Well, apparently, you do. You—you're tangled up in the—whoa, whoa, whoa!" he shouted.

A gust of wind had suddenly dragged a cord from the parachute over to the edge of the roof, causing Phineas, Ferb, and Agent P to trip over it and lose their balance. Then the trio started to fall toward the ground! Luckily, the remaining part of the parachute snagged on a post sticking out of the building, and they were able to safely land on it. "Wow, saved by unconventional architecture!" Phineas exclaimed, once they reached the ground.

Just then, a robot guard that looked suspiciously like Dr. Doofenshmirtz's robot Norm approached them. "May I please see your papers?" he asked politely. Then his voice turned angry. "Show me your papers or be destroyed!"

"Curse you, Perry the Platypus!" both Doofenshmirtzes suddenly howled from above. Then Dr. Doofenshmirtz turned to his alternate evil self and said, "Jinx! You owe me a soda!"

Phineas, Ferb, and Agent P raced down a narrow, dark alley to get away from Norm. The robot looked like he meant business!

"Looks like they're gone," Phineas said as he tried to catch his breath. He looked at Perry again. He still couldn't believe the news about his pet. "You're a secret agent! And you've been living with us this whole time. Was that evil guy right? Were we just a cover story to you? I mean, were you ever really our pet or part of our family? Well, apparently not, because you didn't trust us enough to tell us. Anyone else around here leading a bizarre double life?"

Ferb raised his hand.

"Put your hand down, Ferb!" Phineas snapped. But as Ferb shot him a serious look, he sighed. "You're right, Ferb. We've got to concentrate on the task at hand. We've got to get back to our dimension, and I don't even know where to start."

Phineas reached into his pocket and realized he had the remote control from earlier. "Oh, that's right, the remote! I *knew* that would come in handy! All right, let's go home."

When Phineas pushed a button on the remote, a shimmery portal opened instantly—but it was not a portal back to Danville. He pressed the button again and again and again, but a portal to their own world never appeared.

"Now this thing's broken, and we don't have any tools to fix it," Phineas groaned. "We're going to need some help. Let's go find us." If everyone else had alternate selves, Phineas was sure that he and Ferb had them, too!

Phineas started to lead Ferb and Agent P out of the alley when he suddenly stopped. "Wait, I just realized, you could have been cleaning your own litter box this whole time!" he exclaimed, pointing at Perry. "Oh, we are *not* done with this conversation!"

Then, checking to make sure the coast was clear, Phineas, Ferb, and Agent P ran out of the alley and into the strange new world, where nothing was quite what it seemed.

CHAPTER 4

Back in his evil headquarters, Dr. Doofenshmirtz—2 was in the middle of a little experiment. He held up a picture of Agent P as an undercover agent. "So tell me," he said to Dr. Doofenshmirtz, "what do you see here?"

"An ordinary platypus," Dr. Doofenshmirtz replied.

"And *now* what do you see?" Dr. Doofenshmirtz—2 asked as he displayed another picture of Agent P.

"*Perry* the Platypus!" Dr. Doofenshmirtz gasped.

Dr. Doofenshmirtz—2 shook his head. "You know,

I'm starting to see why you haven't become ruler in your dimension." He strapped Dr. Doofenshmirtz into a school desk and bombarded him with the photos, but Dr. Doofenshmirtz still couldn't tell that they were of the same platypus.

"All right, Mr. Eviler-Than-Thou, just how did you manage to take over the Tri-State Area, anyway?" Dr. Doofenshmirtz asked.

"Simple," Dr. Doofenshmirtz-2 said. "I used an army of big, scary robots."

"We should do lunch sometime," Norm suddenly spoke up in a friendly voice.

"Wow, that *is* scary," Dr. Doofenshmirtz commented. "I tried that robot thing once, too. I hid the self-destruct buttons on the bottom of their feet so no one could reach them. . . ." He closed his eyes at the memory of his beautiful army of robots setting off to take over the Tri-State Area—but with their first steps, each and every one exploded! "I think I've said enough. I *still* don't get it. If we're the same person, why are you so much better at being evil than me?"

"True evil is born through pain and loss," Dr. Doofenshmirtz–2 replied. "You see, when I was a small boy back in Gimelstump, I had a toy train. Then one day, I lost it."

"That's—that's *it*?" asked Dr. Doofenshmirtz.

"What do you mean?" Dr. Doofenshmirtz–2 asked.

"That's your emotionally scarring backstory? *That's* your great tragedy?" Dr. Doofenshmirtz cried. "Dude, I was raised by ocelots. I mean, literally *disowned* by my parents and raised by Central American wildcats. And you're telling me you lost a toy train. That's all? That's all you got? Really? I had to work as a lawn gnome. I was forced to wear hand-me-up girls' clothing. Neither of my parents showed up for my birth!"

"Well, how did you feel when you lost that toy train?" Dr. Doofenshmirtz–2 said.

"I never lost that toy train!" exclaimed Dr. Doofenshmirtz.

"Well, maybe if you had, you'd have done better," Dr. Doofenshmirtz–2 replied. "Since you have neglected to take over *your* Tri-State Area, I think I'll go over there and give it a shot myself."

"Great! We can be a team!" Dr. Doofenshmirtz said excitedly.

"Yeah, right, a team," Dr. Doofenshmirtz–2 replied, rolling his eyes.

"Wait, was that sarcasm?" asked Dr. Doofenshmirtz.

"Noooooo," sneered Dr. Doofenshmirtz–2.

"Yeah, right there—I'm pretty sure that's *my* voice when I'm being sarcastic," Dr. Doofenshmirtz insisted.

For once, Dr. Doofenshmirtz–2 wasn't frustrated by his alternate self's cluelessness. In fact, he found it encouraging.

Maybe taking over the alternate Tri-State Area would be even easier than he'd expected!

Back in Danville, Candace had just arrived at the park, with Stacy, Baljeet, and Isabella trailing behind her. She marched up to Buford. "Okay, Buford, where are Phineas and Ferb?" she demanded.

"How should I know?" Buford replied. "They never showed up for me to return serve. That's considered a forfeit in badminton. So I went to get some victory gum . . . a tradition as old as the game itself."

"Don't play with me, young man," Candace warned. "Where is the giant platypult they built?"

"I don't know," Buford shrugged. "It seems to have vanished."

"Oh, really?" Candace asked as a smug grin crossed her face. "Did you hear that, Stacy? The mysterious force took the platypult away before I, the *grown-up*, could see it!"

"Yeah, yeah," Stacy said with a sigh. "I'm sure there's a *perfectly* logical explanation for all of this."

But there was no way for Stacy to prove that a tow truck had actually carted both platypults away when the kids weren't looking! "And they laughed at me for installing a platypult tow rig," the driver had yelled in victory. "Who's laughing now?"

Candace shook her head. "The logical explanation *is* the mysterious force!" she insisted. "The real question is, why does it care so much about my little brothers? Why doesn't it want them to get busted?"

"Well, why don't you ask it?" Buford sneered.

"Wait, he's right!" Candace realized. "I *should* just ask it! I'll bet I can reason with it!"

"Reason with it?" Stacy asked. "Candace, it's a *force*. That you made up!"

"No, I know what I'm talking about, Stacy. Come on," Candace replied.

"Where are you going?" Stacy asked.

"To my backyard!" Candace yelled over her shoulder as she started to run toward home. "The heart of the mysterious force!"

In the alternate dimension, Phineas, Ferb, and Agent P slowly made their way through the city, trying not to attract attention. They even hid in garbage cans when they had to.

"Well, this should be our street, but it sure looks different," Phineas said as he glanced around. At the same time, he and Ferb noticed someone—someone who looked and walked and talked like their dad, but . . . wasn't.

"Boys, what are you doing here?" Mr. Fletcher–2, their father's alternate-dimension self, said nervously. "You'd better get inside before the Doofbot catches you! I'm off to the factory. See you next week!"

Phineas looked at Ferb with wide eyes. "Wow. Well, I guess we'd better get inside." He turned to Agent P. "You might want to . . . hmm . . . I mean, these guys might not know that you're not really a . . . you know . . ."

Agent P nodded and slipped into his pet disguise at once.

When Phineas rang the doorbell, a woman who looked just like his mom appeared before them. "Boys, I thought you were in your room!" the alternate Mrs. Flynn-Fletcher exclaimed. "Get inside. And get your Dooferalls back on before someone sees you!

If you need me, I'll be hiding in the basement."

Phineas and Ferb exchanged a worried look. "That was weird," Phineas said. "Let's find the other us-es."

The boys and Perry snuck upstairs, where the alternate Phineas and Ferb were playing a board game. "Pick a Doofopoly instruction card," Phineas–2 read. "It says, 'Conform.' I can do that!"

Phineas and Ferb exchanged another glance before they walked into the room. "Hi, guys!" Phineas announced.

"Oh, no, they're replacing us!" Phineas–2 yelped. "I must not have conformed quick enough!"

Phineas–2 and Ferb–2 started bowing to their counterparts.

"No, it's not like that," Phineas said quickly. "We're *you* guys from another dimension."

"Different *dimensions*?" Phineas–2 asked in surprise. "Is that allowed?"

"Apparently," Phineas replied.

Then Phineas–2 spotted Perry. "Oh, look!" he

cried. "Perry's back! Where have you been? We've missed you so much!"

"Uh, Phineas, he's not *your* Perry," Phineas said gently. "He came with us."

"Oh, sorry," Phineas-2 said. "Can I hold him a little longer? It's just that, well, he left one day and never came back. He's been gone for a long time, and I'm really worried."

Right then, their alternate sister, Candace-2, burst into the room. "All right, you know the only time we're allowed to make noise is on Doofensday, so keep it d—" She jumped when she noticed the group. "Are there four of you in this room?" she asked in bewilderment.

"Five, counting Perry," Phineas said helpfully.

"I see nothing," Candace-2 announced as she ran out. "I have plausible deniability."

"Boy, your Candace is much less curious about what you're up to," Phineas said.

"What do you mean?" asked Phineas-2.

"Well, it seems like our Candace has spent her

entire summer focused on what *we're* doing," Phineas explained.

"Summer? I think that was outlawed a long time ago," Phineas–2 said. "It sounds dangerous yet oddly compelling. What is it?"

"What is *summer*?" Phineas asked incredulously. "Man, where do I begin!" He told Phineas–2 and Ferb–2 all about summertime: long days, warm weather, no school, endless time to do cool stuff . . .

"Wow, summer sounds like a blast," Phineas–2 said.

"Oh, yeah," Phineas replied. "That's just the tip of the iceberg. Like this summer, for instance, we built a roller coaster and . . ."

Across the room, the TV played a jaunty jingle: "Doofenshmirtz Evil News Update!" As an image of Dr. Doofenshmirtz–2 flickered over the screen, Perry slipped away from the group to watch.

"This is a message for Other-Dimension Perry the Platypus," the evil doctor announced. "If you turn yourself in, I promise not to hurt your little friends. If you don't, all bets are off."

Perry frowned. It was clear that he had only one option. As he started to creep away, though, Phineas noticed him.

"You are *kidding* me!" Phineas exclaimed. "You're actually sneaking away again? So nothing's changed. Did it ever occur to you that we could help you? That we could have made a great team? But I guess you can't have teamwork without trust. You don't have to sneak away anymore. We know your secret. You can just go."

There was an awkward pause. Then Agent P sadly put on his fedora and slunk away.

The brothers looked at their alternate-dimension counterparts. "I guess if you guys can't help us fix the remote to get back home, we could check with Isabella," Phineas said.

"Who's Isabella?" asked Phineas–2.

"Um, the girl who lives across the street," Phineas replied.

"Mom says that talking to neighbors can be dangerous," said Phineas–2.

51

"It's true!" yelled their alternate mom from the basement.

"Well, it's time you met her," announced Phineas. "Come on, you'll like her!"

"What about the Normbots?" Phineas–2 asked.

"Relax," Phineas told him. "We've been avoiding them all day."

The two Phineases and the two Ferbs crept down the stairs and snuck outside. Phineas tried to reassure everyone as they crossed the street. "If you're really careful, you can—"

Suddenly a Normbot blocked his path!

"Okay, we've got to be more careful than that," Phineas admitted.

"May I please see your identification?" the Normbot requested politely. Then it snarled, "Display your travel papers or be destroyed. Display your travel papers or be . . ."

Suddenly, sparks and wires popped out of the Normbot's head as its circuitry went haywire. Then the robot toppled over and crashed into the street—

revealing an alternate-dimension Buford standing behind it!

"I can't stand these things," Buford–2 complained. He looked at Phineas and Ferb. "Who are *you* guys?"

"We're Candace's brothers," Phineas explained. "We're going to Isabella's."

"Are you part of the resistance?" Phineas–2 asked Buford–2.

"I used to be in the resistance," he replied. "But then I got so good at it that I started resisting *them*."

Phineas's eyes widened when Buford–2 said "resistance." Somewhere, in this strange dimension, there was a secret group of people fighting against Dr. Doofenshmirtz–2.

If he and Ferb could locate them, they might be able to get back home!

CHAPTER 5

Dr. Doofenshmirtz wasted no time building an Other-Dimensionator for his evil counterpart. He was especially eager for Dr. Doofenshmirtz–2's help in taking over the Tri-State Area . . . and just a little desperate to prove that he was actually *very* evil. "Behold, the Other-Dimensionator!" he announced. "Actually, this is the *other* Other-Dimensionator. The Other-Dimensionator is back in the other dimension. Okay, step one is, push this button. Step two, stand back in awe!"

Dr. Doofenshmirtz pressed the button and . . . nothing happened.

"That's it?" asked Dr. Doofenshmirtz–2, raising an eyebrow.

"Er, now that I think about it, those two boys made some modifications to my design which may have allowed it to, you know, work," Dr. Doofenshmirtz admitted.

"Oh, great," Dr. Doofenshmirtz–2 groaned. "Now I need those two boys?"

At that moment, a Normbot burst into the room carrying Agent P, who was all tied up!

"Perry the Platypus!" the two Doofenshmirtzes cackled.

"Listen, Perry the Platypus," Dr. Doofenshmirtz–2 began. "I know I told you if you turned yourself in I wouldn't hurt your friends, but change of plans," he said. "Now I need to hunt them down, which might involve a little hurting. I know that makes me a liar, but, *hello*! Evil!"

Agent P struggled furiously, but not even his

secret-agent training could help him break free of the Normbot's grasp. He'd have to find another way to warn Phineas and Ferb . . . before they were captured!

Meanwhile, Buford–2 was leading the two Phineases and the two Ferbs to Isabella's house. "Come on," he whispered, as he reached out to ring the doorbell. "Isabella's house is right through—*ahhhhhhhhhhhh!*"

As an invisible trapdoor sprang open, the five boys plunged into a hidden lair beneath Isabella's house. A crew of Firestorm Girls captured them instantly.

"Whatcha doin'?" Isabella–2 growled in a tough voice.

"Isabella!" Phineas exclaimed.

"Do I know you?" she asked.

"Hey, Isabella," Buford–2 said.

"Ugh. *Him* I know," Isabella–2 said. "Buford, what do you want? I thought you were resisting us."

"I was helping Candace's brothers cross the street," Buford–2 replied.

"Candace has *two* sets of brothers?" Isabella-2 said in confusion.

"Uh, no," Phineas tried to explain. "He and I are from another dimension. We're trying to get back."

"All right, girls, release them!" Isabella-2 ordered. The Firestorm Girls obeyed. "Why would you want to come to this dimension, anyway?"

"Well, we didn't *mean* to come here," Phineas said. "Now, we can't get back unless we can fix this device."

"We may have someone who can help," Isabella-2 said as she introduced them to a kid who looked very familiar. "Dr. Baljeet."

"Baljeet!" Phineas yelled happily.

"That's *Doctor* Baljeet to you," Baljeet-2 replied. "Were you not listening? Here's the crux of your problem. Think of the universe and all of the many dimensions as circular. The energy flows between the dimensions like this—clockwise. Say this is your dimension, and this is our dimension. You traveled with the flow of energy, so going clockwise would be easy. Going counterclockwise would take eight million gigawatts of energy, overloading the local power grid. Without the eight million gigawatts, you'd have to go clockwise the long way around. Theoretically, you'd get home, but there's no telling how many dimensions you'd have to go through."

"Do you think you can help us get enough power to open the portal backward so we can go home?" asked Phineas.

"Well, we should probably ask our leader," Baljeet-2 said.

Just then, Candace-2 stepped out of the shadows. "Ask your leader *what*?" she snapped.

"Candace, *you're* the leader of the resistance?" Phineas asked in amazement. When he had met Candace-2 earlier, he didn't know that she was in charge of the army!

Frowning, Candace-2 marched up to Phineas-2 and Ferb-2. "What are you two doing here? Never mind, I'll deal with you later." She turned back to Phineas and Ferb. "You two—I've been spending all these years trying to keep my brothers safe, and suddenly their faces are all over the Doofen-channel!"

"We're just trying to get home," Phineas said.

"Well, what's stopping you?" asked Candace–2.

"Right now, quantum physics," Phineas replied.

"We need to generate eight million gigawatts for interdimensional travel," Baljeet–2 reported.

"Then we've got work to do," Candace–2 announced. "Isabella, start redirecting the power. Gretchen, monitor the Doofenchannel," she ordered, pointing to Isabella and one of the Firestorm Girls. "Make sure we're not raising any alarms. Buford, keep resisting."

"No!" Buford–2 argued.

"Excellent," Candace–2 said.

Everyone in the underground lair scurried to work, generating energy on enormous power generators and clicking through a seemingly endless number of portals to other dimensions. Suddenly, they happened upon a world that looked remarkably familiar. In fact, it looked exactly like Phineas and Ferb's backyard in Danville. And the people in it—

"This is going to be the best day ever!" Phineas cheers.

Phineas and his friends build giant *platy*pults
so they can play *platy*pult badminton!

The platypult launches Phineas and Ferb
to Doofenshmirtz Evil, Incorporated!

Dr. Doofenshmirtz has trouble launching his latest -inator.
"I bet we could put this back together in no time," Phineas says.

Dr. Doofenshmirtz's invention transports the gang into a crazy new dimension!

When an evil platyborg tries to attack Phineas and Ferb, Perry reveals that he is a secret agent.

In the new dimension, Dr. Doofenshmirtz meets his alternate
self, who is the leader of the alternate Tri-State Area.

Phineas's and Ferb's alternate selves join the
resistance army to defeat Dr. Doofenshmirtz-2.

"Buford, where are Phineas and Ferb?" Phineas and Ferb's older sister, Candace, asks their friend.

"Perry, if you turn yourself in, I promise not to hurt your friends," warns Dr. Doofenshmirtz-2.

As Perry tries to free his family, a giant monster appears!

After everyone manages to get back to Danville,
Agent P battles an army of robots.

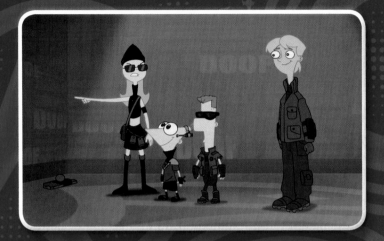

"This is the time to make our move!" Candace's alternate self—the leader of the resistance army—orders.

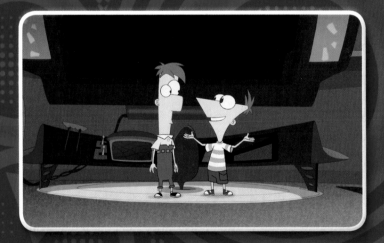

"Ferb, I know what we're going to do today! We're gonna save the Tri-State Area!" Phineas exclaims.

"Now, tremble before me!" Dr. Doofenshmirtz-2 shouts, popping out of a robot.

Everyone wonders if Danville will be saved.

Candace and Stacy—seemed like the *real* Candace and Stacy.

Except Candace was doing something extremely weird. Standing with her arms held out, she chanted, "So, Great and Powerful Mysterious Force, I know you are just trying to protect my brothers. But I am simply trying to protect them, too, from their dangerous inventions. So, show me my brothers!"

But she got no response. Then she had another idea. "Maybe we should build a shrine to it?" Candace whispered.

"Candace, that's ridic—" Stacy began to say.

Suddenly, both girls noticed the shimmery portal! They screamed and ran behind a tree.

"Ferb, I think we got it," Phineas yelled in the other dimension. "It looks like home."

"What do we do now?" Stacy asked Candace.

"I don't know," she replied. "I can't believe it actually worked!"

As Phineas and Ferb prepared to step through the portal, Phineas waved to the members of the resistance. "Well, thanks everyone," he called. "Hey, where's Perry—oh, that's right."

Just then, another Doofenshmirtz Evil News Update blared through the room.

"This just in," a Normbot said on the TV. "Our supreme leader has announced the capture of public enemy number one, Perry the Alternate-Dimension Platypus. I guess we won't be seeing him anymore . . . except as a platyborg. It's three-thirty. We now conclude our broadcast day."

"Now go to bed!" added Dr. Doofenshmirtz–2.

A look of horror crossed Phineas's face. "We've got to save him!"

"Oh, no," Candace–2 said. "Too risky! You've got to get back to your dimension!"

"We're not going anywhere without our platypus," Phineas insisted.

"I thought you told us he was just using you as a cover," said Buford–2.

"I know what I said," Phineas replied. "I was hurt. But even if it was all an act, he's still a part of the family and we're not leaving him behind."

"I may never be able to open this again," Baljeet–2 said as he struggled to keep the portal from closing.

"It doesn't matter," Phineas said firmly. "We're going back for him."

"Well, then, you're on your own!" Candace–2 announced.

"Fine, just tell us where Dr. Doofenshmirtz keeps his prisoners," Phineas said.

Candace–2 shook her head.

Then Phineas–2 spoke up. "We have to help them."

"Oh, no, we don't," argued Candace–2.

"Yes, we do! Remember how we felt when *our* Perry disappeared?" Phineas–2 asked her.

Candace–2 looked at her brothers. Their sad eyes made her pause. "Oh, criminy, I must be crazy," she said with a groan. "All right, we can get there through the tunnels. Let's suit up, people!"

At the same time, in Danville, Candace found the courage to approach the portal to the other dimension. Through it, she could see Phineas and Ferb. "You know what, Stacy?" she said. "I'm tired of the mysterious force pushing me around. I'm going to show it who's boss!"

"Candace, wait!" Stacy cried.

But once Candace had made up her mind, nothing could stop her. She took a deep breath as she psyched herself up to jump through the portal.

Baljeet–2 stood on the other side, doing everything he could to protect the portal. "I will try to keep it open as long as possible, but it is very unstable," he warned Phineas. "Even the slightest disturbance will cause it to collapse."

Baljeet–2 had barely finished speaking when suddenly Candace barreled through the portal and landed in a heap on the floor!

"Like that, for instance," Baljeet–2 sighed as the portal vanished.

"Hey, Candace!" Phineas exclaimed.

Candace dusted herself off and stormed over to Phineas. "You guys are so—wait, why are there four of you?" she asked, looking at the two Phineases and two Ferbs in confusion.

"Oh, these guys are from *this* dimens—" Phineas began.

"Are we inside the mysterious force?" Candace gasped.

"I'm not sure I understand the ques—" Phineas started to say.

"And why is Isabella suddenly fashionable?" Candace asked, looking at Isabella–2's beret, T-shirt, and cargo pants.

"What do you mean, 'suddenly'?" Isabella–2 asked, frowning.

"Seriously, where are we?" Candace said.

"Candace, I'm sure you have a million questions, but right now we've got to save Perry from being turned into a cyborg!" Phineas told her.

Candace looked at him strangely. "What?"

"We'll explain on the way," Phineas promised.

"So how *do* I dress in your dimension?" Isabella–2 asked Candace.

But Candace didn't answer. She'd caught a glimpse of Candace-2, and her mouth dropped open. "Hey, is that *me*?" she exclaimed. "I look *good*!"

As Candace admired her alternate-dimension self, Phineas and Ferb grabbed her shoulders to steer her in the other direction. Phineas-2 and Ferb-2 tried to follow them—but Candace-2 blocked their way. "Oh, no, you two stay here," she said firmly.

"But we want to help!" Phineas-2 cried.

"That's an order," Candace-2 told them.

She stood there with her hands on her hips until Phineas-2 and Ferb-2 gave up. Candace-2 could tell that they were disappointed, but there wasn't anything she could do about that. She knew just how serious—and dangerous—this mission would be.

The only way to keep her brothers safe was to forbid them from coming.

CHAPTER 6

Candace–2 led the group to a hidden underground cavern, where they climbed into mine cars perched on rickety tracks. With a sudden *whoosh*, the cars raced off, barreling through the darkness.

If she hadn't been so preoccupied with trying to figure out this strange new world, Candace would have been terrified. Luckily, she had other things on her mind. "Wait, so in this dimension, Perry is a secret agent?" she asked Phineas.

"No, in this dimension, he's a cyborg," Phineas told her.

"So, where is he an agent?" Candace asked.

"That would be our dimension," Phineas explained patiently. "But we're not *in* our dimension now."

"Okay, I'm having a little trouble processing this," said Candace.

"Now I wish I hadn't thrown away that pamphlet," Phineas commented.

"And why are we in mine cars?" Candace asked.

"They'll take us as far as the underground entrance to Doof's headquarters," Isabella–2 reported.

Candace–2 opened a map and showed it to Phineas. "From there, we go up the ventilation shaft," she said. "The detainment center is on level four."

"The snack bar's on level five . . . if there's time," Buford–2 said hopefully. Candace–2 looked at him and frowned. "I'm just going to get some nachos!" he said defensively.

Candace–2 rolled her eyes. Then she noticed that Candace was looking at her curiously.

"So, if there's another *me* and another *them*, theeeeeen . . . there must also be a Jeremy Johnson here, too, right?" Candace asked hopefully.

"Huh?" Candace–2 asked. "Oh, yeah, Johnson, Jeremy. Leads a three-man strike team on the north side. Good soldier."

"Good soldier?" repeated Candace. "That's *all* you think of him? Don't you think he's dreamy? Or cool? Or even *cute*? Tell me at least you think he's cute."

"Cute doesn't win the war, kid," Candace–2 replied.

"Oh, well, I guess . . ." Candace said slowly. "But what do you guys do around here for, you know, for fun?"

Candace–2 sighed. "Look . . . Candace, is it? No offense, but fun isn't really on my agenda. You know, ever since Doofenshmirtz took over the Tri-State Area, even though I was a little girl, I've been focused on one thing and one thing only. He's going down, down, down!"

"Down, down, down, I know," Candace interrupted.

"But what about BFFs or slumber parties? Or busting your little brothers?"

"Busting my little brothers?" Candace–2 repeated. "I spend every day of my life trying to protect my little brothers. I had to grow up pretty quick around here to make sure they didn't have to."

"Gee, you make growing up sound like it's a bad thing," Candace said.

"It is what it is," Candace–2 said with a shrug. "I'd do whatever it takes to protect the ones I love."

At that moment, Phineas–2 and Ferb–2 popped out from under a tarp covering one of the cars! "Aw, thanks, Sis," Phineas–2 said, grinning.

"What are you doing here?" yelled Candace–2.

"We're here to help," Phineas–2 replied.

"We're nearing the target," Isabella–2 reported.

"Ugh," Candace–2 groaned. She turned to her brothers. "Don't move," she ordered. Then she grabbed the controls and brought the cars to a stop.

"Okay, people, change of plans," she announced as she handed Phineas the map. "This is as far as we go."

"We're not going to help them?" asked Phineas–2.

"No, *we're* going to get you two home where it's safe," Candace–2 replied.

"But we want to—" her brother started to say.

"Look, this isn't our fight," Candace–2 told him. "It's *their* fight, and you two shouldn't have gotten involved. Maybe none of us should have." She pushed open the door so that Phineas, Ferb, and Candace could get out. "There. Now we're out of here."

Buford–2 glanced around nervously. "I don't remember it being so dark down here."

"Dark?" Candace–2 echoed.

"That's because it's a trap!" Dr. Doofenshmirtz's voice rang out as he turned on the lights. "Ha-ha! And if it was light, you would have seen us and run away, hence ruining the trap!"

"I think they get that," Dr. Doofenshmirtz–2 said. He held on to a heavy chain that was clamped around Agent P's neck.

"Perry!" Phineas cried joyfully when he saw his pet.

"We, uh, we, uh, well, we came to rescue you. So far it's not going as well as we'd hoped. We didn't have a lot of time to, you know, plan something more elaborate, but I guess we could've created some sort of diversion . . . just in case." He sighed. "Yeah, we could have thought this out more."

Dr. Doofenshmirtz—2 laughed. "I got you, and I got your little friends, too! Game over! You lose, I win! Mark this the hour of your doom, Perry the Platypus. Three-forty—oh!" he cried suddenly. "I got one of those watches with just little hash marks. It doesn't even have numbers on it. Wait—let's just say it's between three-thirty and four o'clock."

Hearing the time gave Agent P an idea. He aimed his watch at the two Doofenshmirtzes and pressed a button. A hologram of Major Monogram—soaking wet and covered in bubbles—suddenly appeared.

"Whoa! I told you! Not between three-thirty and four!" Major Monogram yelled from the shower.

"Ahhhhhhhhhh!" screamed Dr. Doofenshmirtz—2. The blinding brightness of the hologram made him drop the chain, just as Agent P had hoped it would.

"Run!" Phineas yelled.

Everyone did as they were instructed.

"They're getting away!" Dr. Doofenshmirtz−2 howled.

"Go-go-go-go-go-go!" shouted Candace−2 as she helped the kids into the mine cars. "Isabella, start the motor!"

"Yes, sir!" Isabella−2 replied. "I got it."

The mine cars leaped down the track, just as an entire army of robots appeared!

"You two, keep your heads down and remember your training!" Candace−2 told her brothers.

"We never *had* any training!" Phineas−2 replied.

"Well, keep your heads down. Consider yourself trained. This is going to be close," she said, grabbing a metal pole. "All right, you rust buckets, let's dance!" she yelled to the robots.

Candace−2 started whipping the pole through the air like a martial-arts master, knocking out robots right and left.

Phineas looked at his sister with wide eyes. "Can *you* do that?"

"Well, apparently," she replied. But even Candace looked impressed with her alternate self's moves!

"If we can get to the north tunnel before they get to us, I can trip the security door!" Candace–2 shouted. "Isabella, can you give us more throttle?"

"It's all the way in, sir," replied Isabella–2.

"All right, hang tough," Candace–2 said. "This is going to get hairy."

"Can we make those turns at this speed?" Isabella–2 asked.

"Well, we're about to find out," Candace–2 said grimly as she flipped a switch. Suddenly, the cars veered onto a different track, rounding the corner on only two wheels! Candace–2 pushed the engine to its limits while Phineas, Ferb, and Agent P battled the robots from the last car.

"There it is," she yelled, pointing ahead at the entrance to the tunnel. "We should be okay if we can hold off these—"

Candace–2's voice trailed off as robots all around her were blasted to pieces. She looked around and discovered that Phineas and Ferb were using the robot's arm to shoot at the other attackers!

"Can *we* do that?" Phineas–2 asked, in awe.

"No!" barked Candace–2. "Keep your head down!"

Suddenly, the platyborg arrived! It shot off the back wheel of the car, which made Phineas drop the robot arm he was using as a weapon. The damaged wheel dragged along the track. The platyborg stood on the tracks, satisfied with what it had accomplished.

"We're slowing down, sir!" Isabella–2 shouted.

"Keep it on the floor!" Candace–2 ordered her.

"It's *on* the floor," Isabella–2 cried. "There's too much drag. I don't think we're going to make it."

"Everyone, to the front, now!" Candace–2 shouted. "We're going to have to cut loose these cars—"

Suddenly, the middle car burst into flames, separating Phineas, Ferb, Candace, and Agent P from the rest of the group!

"Whoa!" Phineas yelled.

"The motor's overheating!" Isabella–2 cried.

Candace–2 looked at the sparks flying from the motor and the burning car. She only had an instant to make a difficult decision. "Sorry, guys, you're on your own," she said.

Then Candace–2 knocked out the pin connecting the cars. Her car sped away—leaving Phineas, Ferb, Candace, and Agent P behind!

"What are you doing?" Phineas–2 gasped.

"My job," she replied. "Protecting you two."

"We've got to go back to help them!" Phineas–2 yelled urgently.

"That's not our fight," Candace–2 said.

"But you just abandoned them!" Phineas–2 cried. "We could have made it. We could have *all* made it!"

"Or we could have all been captured, and I wasn't going to take that chance," Candace–2 argued. "These are the tough choices. Somebody's got to be the adult here—you two are safe, and that's what's important."

"But—but—but—" her brother protested.

"End of discussion!" Candace–2 interrupted him.

There was nothing that Phineas–2 could do but watch as the robots descended on Phineas, Ferb, Candace, and Agent P. Like it or not, it looked as if the real Phineas, Ferb, Candace, and Agent P were on their own.

CHAPTER 7

Stacy could hardly believe it: Candace had simply disappeared! One minute Stacy was teasing Candace about believing in a "mysterious force"—and the next minute it had swallowed up her best friend. Trying to explain this to an adult would be hopeless, Stacy knew. She could only think of one thing to do.

Stacy got right to work. First, she got a thick roll of police tape and wrapped it around the spot where Candace had vanished. Then she started building the altar that Candace had suggested they make earlier.

Stacy gathered everything she could think of as an offering—or bribe: flowers in every color, all kinds of fruit, and several electric candles. Finally, Stacy added the most important offering of all—Candace's teddy bear, Mr. Miggins. Then she knelt in front of the altar, threw out her arms, and stared at the sky.

"Look, Mysterious Force," Stacy began nervously, "I feel a little awkward talking to you since . . . I didn't believe in you at first, cause, you know, it's crazy. But then I saw you . . . eat . . . my . . . friend, so I've made a little shrine here. It's uh . . . it's nice. There's a banana, and, oh, oh, oooh, Mr. Miggins! So I, uh, hope this makes up for the whole 'disbelief' thing. Are we, uh . . . are we good?"

Stacy sat down and waited for a sign from the mysterious force. Nothing happened at first, but Stacy was patient. She would wait as long as it took to get Candace back.

Underground in the alternate dimension, Phineas,

Ferb, Candace, and Agent P fought as hard as they could, but they were so outnumbered by the robot army that their surrender was inevitable. The giant robots swooped down, picked them up, and whisked them off to a meeting with both Dr. Doofenshmirtzes. Dr. Doofenshmirtz–2 smiled evilly when everyone arrived in his lair.

"Now you have no choice but to fix my machine!" he cried.

"No," Phineas said.

"Fix the machine!" Dr. Doofenshmirtz–2 snapped. He meant business.

"No," repeated Phineas.

"Can, uh, can I say something?" Candace asked anxiously. "So I think I'm up to date on the whole Perry 'agent' thing; strangely, that's the most normal thing that's happened this afternoon. But who exactly is *this* guy?" she asked, looking at Dr. Doofenshmirtz–2.

"Fix it!" bellowed Dr. Doofenshmirtz–2.

"No!" Phineas replied.

Dr. Doofenshmirtz—2 sighed. "Look, I would make myself do it, but apparently *he's* an idiot," he said, pointing to his alternate self.

"Hey!" Dr. Doofenshmirtz protested.

"Fix the machine!" Dr. Doofenshmirtz—2 ordered again.

"No!" Phineas told him.

"All right then, you've forced me to bring out the big guns," Dr. Doofenshmirtz—2 sneered as he pulled a sock puppet onto his hand. He spoke in a squeaky voice. "Fix the machine."

"No," Phineas repeated.

"*Really*?" Dr. Doofenshmirtz—2 said in surprise. "When I was your age, I did anything a puppet told me to."

"How old do you think we are?" Phineas asked.

"I don't know, one, two?" Dr. Doofenshmirtz—2 guessed. "It's, uh, you know, it's hard to tell with the one eye. Anyway, I don't know why you're being so uncooperative. All I'm asking you to do is to make my machine work so I can invade and conquer your world and enslave your loved ones."

"See, that's just it," Phineas began to explain. "Why would we do something that would lead to our own self-destruction?"

Dr. Doofenshmirtz's eyes lit up. At last, he'd figured out a way to be helpful! "Self-destruction?" he yelled. "Wait, wait, that's it! I remember now! They—they took out my self-destruct button! I don't know why I put it back in, but here, I'll just rewire this like so, aaand—there! It's working! It's working! It's functioning properly!"

"Well, look who just became redundant," Dr. Doofenshmirtz–2 said. He stared at Phineas and Ferb. "Send them to their doom! Yes, her, too. Doom, doom, doom and . . . doom!"

"Doom!" Dr. Doofenshmirtz said at the same time. "Jinx!"

"Okay, doom for him, too," Dr. Doofenshmirtz–2 said, sounding bored.

"What?" Dr. Doofenshmirtz gasped. "But—but I'm *you!*"

Dr. Doofenshmirtz—2 shook his head. He then made his puppet yell, "Doooooooooooom!"

"Wow, if I had a nickel for every time I was doomed by a puppet, I'd have two nickels," Dr. Doofenshmirtz marveled. "Which isn't a lot, but it's weird that it happened twice, right?"

Before anyone could respond, the robots descended in a storm of clanking metal. They shackled all the prisoners—including Dr. Doofenshmirtz—and marched them outside while Dr. Doofenshmirtz—2 took the express elevator. He was waiting for them at the mouth of a deep pit that was surrounded by lawn gnomes.

"Welcome, doomed guests!" Dr. Doofenshmirtz—2 cried gleefully. "Come on, keep trudging. Doom is that-away!"

"I would say, so far adulthood gets about a three," Candace grumbled.

"You know, this may be as good as it gets," Dr. Doofenshmirtz told her.

"And now, for my all-time favorite game . . . Poke the Goozim with a Stick, surrounded by lava!" Dr.

Doofenshmirtz-2 announced. "Followed very closely by backgammon. Love it!"

Then the prisoners caught a glimpse of what was lurking in the pit: a huge, snarling monster in a cage—the Goozim!

"Whoa, whoa, hold the phone!" Dr. Doofenshmirtz said in a panic. "I could be useful. What if you need a kidney? Or a stand-in for boring functions you have to attend? Or another kidney?"

"Dooooooooooooom!" shouted Dr. Doofenshmirtz-2.

The Goozim roared loudly as one of the robots started cranking open its cage.

"I'll be honest, Ferb," Phineas said. "I'm having a hard time putting a positive spin on this."

"Yeah, well, welcome to my life," Dr. Doofenshmirtz said.

Phineas's eyes narrowed as he noticed two things: Perry had quietly slipped out of his chains, and a nearby robot had the keys that could set the rest of them free. "Perry, check out that guard," he whispered. "Keys!"

Agent P nodded. He activated his watch's electro-magnetic beam, which zapped the keys right off the guard's belt!

"Cool!" Phineas exclaimed as Agent P unlocked his shackles. But when the robot realized that Agent P had the keys, it lunged at him! "Ahhh! Look out!"

"Is *this* the plan?" Dr. Doofenshmirtz asked. "Ahhhh! Tell me this isn't the plan!"

As soon as he was out of his shackles, Ferb leaped onto the Normbot, opened up its control panel, and fiddled with the wires.

"You are tampering with the property of Doctor—let's make omelettes!" the Normbot said as it started to malfunction.

Suddenly, everyone except Dr. Doofenshmirtz-2 pitched over and fell onto the Goozim's cage! The beast roared angrily and rattled the bars so much that the door fell off and plunged into the bubbling lava.

"Yes! Go, Goozim!" cheered Dr. Doofenshmirtz-2.

"It's muffin time, sir!" announced the Normbot.

"Already?" Dr. Doofenshmirtz–2 asked. He shrugged his shoulders, accepted a muffin from the Normbot, and started to eat it.

As the Goozim charged ahead, the prisoners—who were still partly chained together—leaped off the cage roof. Then something terrible happened. Agent P dropped the keys! Thinking fast, Candace miraculously grabbed them before they dropped into the lava.

"Oh, great! You caught them!" Dr. Doofenshmirtz exclaimed. "Unlock me!"

"Are you even paying attention?" Candace screamed as she pointed at the approaching Goozim.

"Oh, that's right. It can wait," Dr. Doofenshmirtz replied.

Dr. Doofenshmirtz–2 spat out a bite of muffin when he realized the Goozim was free. "More guards!" he ordered.

But the malfunctioning Normbot just offered him another muffin. "It's muffin time, sir," the robot said again and again.

"You're broken!" Dr. Doofenshmirtz–2 realized.

Phineas glanced from the smoking lava to the furious Goozim to an approaching army of robot guards. The only thing keeping the group out of the lava was Perry, who was hanging on to the cage with all his strength. Phineas had a feeling that they might not make it out of this mess.

Then something astonishing and completely unexpected happened: Candace–2 arrived to rescue them!

"Yay, Other-Dimension Candace!" Phineas exclaimed.

"Phineas! Catch!" Candace–2 screamed as she threw something toward him.

"The remote!" he shouted. "Perry, let go!"

"What?" shrieked Candace. "No, no! Don't let go!"

Phineas looked at Perry. "Perry, trust me," Phineas urged.

"Two words: La *Va*," Candace replied, pointing at the oozing, bubbling fire below.

"Trust me," Phineas insisted.

Perry nodded. He let go, and everyone plummeted

toward the pit of lava, screaming at the top of their lungs!

Then Phineas punched a button on the remote, and a portal to another dimension opened beneath them! Instead of falling into the lava, the prisoners plunged into a new dimension that was full of . . . pretty flowers.

To everyone's horror, the Goozim followed them, but somehow interdimensional travel made it lose all of its mangy fur. Now the beast was nothing more than a scrawny, wrinkly dog. It ran off, whimpering with embarrassment.

"They opened another portal!" howled Dr. Doofenshmirtz-2 from back in his lair. "Go after them!" he told the Normbot.

Candace-2 suddenly swung past Dr. Doofenshmirtz-2, destroying groups of robots.

"And her—get her, too!" he added.

In the flower dimension, Agent P unlocked everyone's shackles—even Dr. Doofenshmirtz's.

"Thanks, Perry the Platypus," he said gratefully.

Suddenly, a crew of Normbots began to stream through the portal!

"Stop where you are! You cannot leave!" one robot barked.

"I use aggression to mask my insecurities!" announced another.

"The portal!" Phineas gasped as he pointed the remote and closed it—but not before a few more Normbots got through. They were the lucky ones. Back in the other dimension, the other Normbots fell into the lava as soon as Phineas shut the portal!

As lasers blasted all around them, Phineas knew that there was only one way to escape: by opening another portal.

"Okay, follow me!" he yelled. "We're going around clockwise!"

"Whoa, whoa, *whoaaaaaa*!" everyone screamed as they fell through a new portal.

"The portal closed, sir," one of the Normbots reported to Dr. Doofenshmirtz–2, while another one captured Candace–2.

"Oh, well, time to start the invasion!" Dr. Doofenshmirtz–2 announced. "And somebody get me a muffin!"

"But it's not muffin time, sir," a Normbot replied.

But that didn't bother Dr. Doofenshmirtz–2. After all, he had bigger things on his mind. Like launching a full-scale invasion of another Tri-State Area. Finally, his dreams of complete Tri-State Area domination were about to come true!

CHAPTER 8

In the evilest room of his headquarters, Dr. Doofenshmirtz–2 fired up the Other-Dimensionator. He hadn't been this excited since the *last* time he had conquered a Tri-State Area. "Ha-ha-ha-ha-ha!" he cackled as his robot army assembled around him. "I spy with my one little eye a *new* Tri-State Area that's one dictator short of a dictatorship! But that's all about to change. Pretty soon, I'll be ruling over *two* Tri-State Areas, a virtual six-state area! It's unprecedented, really."

With a triumphant laugh, Dr. Doofenshmirtz–2 opened the portal, and his robots began the invasion.

Back in the park in Danville, Buford, Baljeet, and Isabella were still waiting for Phineas and Ferb to return.

Suddenly, a portal opened up right in front of them! Phineas, Ferb, Candace, Dr. Doofenshmirtz, and Agent P tumbled through it.

"Wait, I think this is it," Phineas said hopefully.

"Where have you guys been?" Isabella asked.

"This *is* it!" Phineas announced.

"Why is Perry wearing a hat?" Baljeet wondered aloud.

"We don't have time to explain," Phineas said. "We've got to try to stop an evil—"

But at that moment, swarms of robots poured out of a new portal that had just opened over the headquarters of Doofenshmirtz Evil, Incorporated.

"Uh-oh, it's too late!" Candace cried.

All over town, people panicked as the robots descended and began to attack—smashing buildings, throwing cars, and blasting lasers all over Danville!

Just then, a hologram of Major Monogram appeared out of Perry's watch.

"Agent P, our agents are being overwhelmed by the sheer number of robots coming into our dimension," Major Monogram said gravely. "You must get to Dr. Doofenshmirtz's headquarters and stop them!"

"Aye-aye, sir, we're ready to serve," Phineas said as he saluted the commander.

"Nope. Far too dangerous," Major Monogram replied, shaking his head.

"Perry?" Phineas asked. He knew his pet wouldn't let him down.

But Agent P yanked off the locket Phineas and Ferb had given him five years ago and handed it back to them.

"Wow, I guess we're going home then," Phineas said sadly.

As Phineas and Ferb trudged away, Agent P's shoulders fell. He hated that he had disappointed his owners.

Meanwhile, Dr. Doofenshmirtz was racing off to his headquarters to find a way to close the portal. But when he got there, he realized that he'd lost his keys—*and* the door was locked! One of his neighbors would have to let him in. He pressed a button on the intercom.

"Hello?" a voice said.

"Hello, Mrs. Thompson?" he asked politely. "It's Heinz. I think I left my keys in the other dimension. Can you buzz me in?"

"Who is this?" Mrs. Thompson asked suspiciously.

"Heinz Doofenshmirtz. Your neighbor. For, like, twelve years," he said, trying to stay calm.

"*Who*?" asked Mrs. Thompson.

Dr. Doofenshmirtz buried his head in his hands. Getting into his building might take a little longer than he first expected. The only problem was that he was running out of time!

Back in the alternate dimension, Candace–2 found

herself locked in a tiny prison cell. "Oh, this is just beautiful," she said sarcastically. "I decide to do the right thing, and I end up in a cell. What lesson am I supposed to be learning here?"

Suddenly, there was a loud clatter by the bars. Candace–2 jumped up as the door slammed open.

"I'm Jeremy Johnson," a tall, blond-haired boy announced. "I'm here to rescue you!"

"Johnson? Jeremy?" she asked. That name sounded familiar. . . .

"Yes, sir." Jeremy–2 saluted. "And I picked up a couple of new recruits."

Just then, Phineas–2 and Ferb–2 burst into the cell. "We found a way to bypass the entire security grid level by level. It was cool!" Phineas–2 exclaimed.

"What?" Candace–2 spun around to face Jeremy–2. "You brought my little brothers? Are you out of your *mind*, soldier?" She couldn't believe it! Her brothers were decked out in resistance gear, and looked like they meant business.

"I didn't know they were your brothers," Jeremy–2

replied. "But I should've known. They're smart and courageous, just like you."

"You think I'm smart and courageous?" Candace–2 asked.

"Well, yeah," Jeremy–2 said. "Uh, sir."

"Uh . . . good work, soldier," she said awkwardly.

"We should really get out of here while we can," Jeremy–2 said as he glanced over his shoulder. "Most of the Normbots are in the other dimension. We can slip away pretty easily."

"The *Normbots* are in the other *dimension*?" Candace–2 asked. "This isn't the time to escape. This is the time to make our move. Let's go!"

"Yes, sir," everyone responded.

"Boys, wait," Candace–2 suddenly said. "Thanks for rescuing me. I'm really proud of you both."

"And we're proud of you, too," Phineas–2 replied, adding, "Sir!"

Then Buford–2 strolled into the jail cell. "I've got nachos! Who wants some?" he asked. "Nobody?" he said in surprise, loudly crunching on a handful of chips.

In Danville, Phineas, Ferb, and Candace didn't speak as they hurried toward home, hiding from robots behind trash cans and trees. In the backyard, they found Stacy bowing before the altar she'd built.

"Oh, Mysterious Force, you can see I'm *really* trying here!" Stacy begged. "Please bring back Candace!"

"Oh, hi, Stacy," Candace said.

Stacy's eyes widened as she realized that Candace was standing next to her! She immediately squeezed her eyes shut again. "And I also want a car!" she said, crossing her fingers.

Phineas and Ferb went inside, where they flopped down on the couch and turned on the TV. An emergency news broadcast was on every channel.

"There are robots all over the Tri-State Area!" the anchor said breathlessly. "And now for the weather."

The camera panned over to the weatherman, who

was in a total panic. "Robots, Phil!" he screamed. "Robots!"

Beep!

Phineas and Ferb looked at each other.

Beep!

"Ferb . . . do you hear that?" Phineas asked, reaching into his pocket. "It's Perry's locket. Ohhh, it's like a homing device!"

The locket led them to a picture hanging on the wall. When Phineas moved it, he discovered that there was a hole behind it.

"Shall we?" Phineas asked excitedly.

Phineas and Ferb crawled through the hole and dropped right into Agent P's chair—in the middle of his secret chamber!

"This must be Perry's lair," Phineas realized.

"Welcome, Phineas and Ferb," a computerized voice said. "Please insert the key."

"Do you have the key?" Phineas asked Ferb as he peered at the keyhole. "That's an oddly shaped keyhole. It kind of looks like . . . Wait a minute. . . ."

Phineas carefully positioned Perry's locket in the keyhole. It was a perfect fit!

"Phineas and Ferb, this message is top secret: for your ears only," the computer voice announced. "If you are hearing this, the Tri-State Area is at emergency-alert level alpha red. Agent P needs your help."

"How does he know *we'll* know what to do?" asked Phineas.

"He knows you will know what to do," the voice replied. "He also knows you two are the only ones capable of helping him. Because you two are the only ones capable of creating these . . ."

Suddenly, several doors *whooshed* open to reveal amazing contraptions in all shapes and sizes. They were all of Phineas and Ferb's inventions!

"Ferb, I know what we're gonna do today!" Phineas exclaimed.

Grabbing all their inventions, Phineas and Ferb raced out of Perry's lair, where robots were storming the streets of Danville. They knew they had to find Perry as fast as possible—and they knew that he would most likely be in the heart of the action, near the headquarters of Doofenshmirtz Evil, Incorporated.

Just a few streets away, Agent P was looking for the secret agents that needed his help. He was not about to let them down!

As Agent P approached the downtown area, he realized how right Major Monogram was. His fellow agents were being defeated—badly. Agent P drew on all his years of training as he entered the fight, walloping robot after robot—until one determined Normbot trapped him! Agent P struggled to get free, but the Normbot wouldn't budge.

Suddenly, a stream of flying baseballs whacked the Normbot right in the face! Phineas had arrived—and he was putting his baseball gun to good use.

"We've got to do something about that portal," Phineas yelled as Agent P escaped from the Normbot. "Ferb! We're going to try to close that portal!"

Agent P fired a grappling hook onto the top floor of Doofenshmirtz Evil, Incorporated. Then Phineas and Agent P rode the grappling hook all the way to the balcony while Ferb stayed behind to battle more robots. Right away, they spotted Dr. Doofenshmirtz–2 looming in the portal—but the platyborg blocked their way! Agent P fought the platyborg so Phineas could throw the grappling hook at the portal. Unfortunately, Dr. Doofenshmirtz–2 heard the *ping* as the hook made contact. An evil scowl crossed his face when he saw Phineas climbing the rope toward him.

"What? Oh!" he yelled as he grabbed a piece of peanut brittle, his favorite candy, and threw it at Phineas. It severed the rope, dropping Phineas back onto the balcony. He bounced off Dr. Doofenshmirtz's old couch and leaped to his feet.

"I've had just about enough of you!" Dr. Doofenshmirtz–2 yelled as he jumped through the portal, landing on the roof of his alternate self's evil headquarters.

Phineas had to think fast. He grabbed the couch cushion that Perry had peed on and shoved it in Dr. Doofenshmirtz–2's face!

Dr. Doofenshmirtz–2 cried out in disgust as he

tried to pry the pillow off of him. "Oh, what is *on* this!"

Phineas knew that it would take more than a pee-soaked cushion to stop Dr. Doofenshmirtz–2. He raced over to help Agent P battle the platyborg.

If there was any hope of saving the Tri-State Area, they would have to do it together. It was now or never!

CHAPTER 9

Back at the Flynn-Fletcher house, Candace and Stacy watched as tons of robots marched in the street.

"I was wrong, Stacy, about everything," Candace said with a sigh. "I'm *not* a grown-up. I can't fight giant robots. I can't control mysterious forces. I can't even get my mom to see what my brothers are doing."

The girls stood in silence for a moment, until Candace gasped so loudly that it made Stacy jump. "Stacy, that's *it*!" she cried. "I can't get my mom to see what my brothers are doing!"

"Huh?" Stacy asked in confusion.

"I'm going to bust my brothers to my mom—and I'm going to *fail*!" Candace yelled as she ran toward the movie theater where her parents were.

Meanwhile, Dr. Doofenshmirtz–2's master control panel began to malfunction, and all the robots started going haywire. "Eh, come on, ya stupid thing, *work*!" Dr. Doofenshmirtz–2 yelled as he smacked at the antenna.

Hiding behind a column, Phineas watched the whole scene. "So that dish must be what's controlling the robots . . ." he realized.

Downstairs, Dr. Doofenshmirtz was still begging Mrs. Thompson to buzz him in. "No, it's Heinz *Doofenshmirtz*," he said again. "You borrowed sugar from me this morning."

"Sorry, I don't have any sugar," Mrs. Thompson said over the intercom. "I had to borrow some from my neighbor this morning."

Dr. Doofenshmirtz jumped up in excitement. "Yeah, that's me!" he cried.

"He's a nice man, but I hear he's divorced," Mrs. Thompson continued.

"Oh, *that* she remembers," Dr. Doofenshmirtz groaned as he banged his head against the locked door.

Meanwhile, Candace had just reached the movie theater, where robots were stomping in the aisles. She found her parents sitting near the back, wearing 3-D glasses.

"Psst!" Candace hissed. "Mom! Mom!"

"Candace, what are you doing here?" her mother asked, without taking her eyes off the screen.

"You've got to come outside and bust the boys!" Candace replied.

"I'm not leaving now!" her mom argued. "The girl is about to forgive the guy for the cliché misunderstanding. Well, after she battles these robots."

"Wow! This 3-D is amazing!" Candace's dad marveled. Her parents thought the robots in the theater were actually part of the movie!

Candace was so frustrated that she almost threw

a temper tantrum. She clenched her fists and took a deep breath.

She was determined to get her mom out of that theater—even if she had to drag her into the street!

At Doofenshmirtz Evil, Incorporated, Agent P was in the middle of a furious fight with the platyborg. The mutated creature was just about to push him over the edge of the building when Agent P had a brilliant idea: he remembered the universal platypus tickle spot!

He could only hope that the platyborg still had one.

Agent P started tickling the platyborg, whose tail flapped back and forth as it squirmed. Agent P tickled it right across the balcony—not far from where Phineas was trying to grab his baseball gun.

"Oh, no, you don't!" Dr. Doofenshmirtz–2 shouted as he reached for the device. "Now the baseball is on the other foot . . . or however that saying goes. I'm not really sure. . . . Hey, hey, where are you going? You know all that's going to happen from you guys coming up here is that I'll have a brand-new platyborg, and maybe even a boy-borg, too."

A loud sizzle and a shower of sparks interrupted him. Dr. Doofenshmirtz-2 realized that Agent P had tickled the platyborg into an electrical circuit, crossing its wires for good!

Agent P used his tail to knock a baseball bat over to Phineas. Phineas grabbed it and crouched into a batter's stance, knowing that this was the most important swing he'd ever take.

Narrowing his eyes, Dr. Doofenshmirtz-2 aimed the baseball gun at Phineas and fired. Phineas was ready for him. He swung the bat as hard as he could and—

Crack!

The bat whacked the baseball and sent it flying right back at Dr. Doofenshmirtz-2! There was nothing the evil scientist could do to keep it from smashing the antenna controlling his entire robot army!

"Noooooooooo!" howled Dr. Doofenshmirtz–2 as the robots started falling from the sky. "Oh, no! Oh, my babies! No! What have you done!"

Meanwhile, Dr. Doofenshmirtz tried once more to convince Mrs. Thompson to let him in. "Hello? I'm selling magazines," he said, slumping against the door.

Bzzzzzzzzzzzzz!

"Come on up!" Mrs. Thompson called as she buzzed him in.

Over at the movie theater, Candace grabbed her mom's shoulders. "Mom, if you love me, if you care *one* iota about me, your family, and your city, you'll come outside with me right now!" she exclaimed.

"Well, I guess I could use some more popcorn," her mom said slowly. "Okay."

"Great!" Candace replied. "C'mon, c'mon, c'mon, c'mon!"

At Doofenshmirtz Evil, Incorporated, Ferb arrived on the balcony.

"Ferb, bro!" Phineas yelled. "I just hit the best home run ever!"

But before the boys could celebrate, the ground started to shake. Suddenly, a giant robot burst out of the concrete!

"Now, tremble before me!" Dr. Doofenshmirtz—2 commanded from inside the robot's sleeve. "You didn't know I had another trick up my sleeve, did you? It's me! *I'm* the trick up my own sleeve, because I'm in the sleeve. Hope you've got your 3-D glasses, 'cause I'm *comin' at'cha!*"

Phineas, Ferb, and Agent P exchanged a worried glance. How could they ever defeat such an enormous robot?

"Hey, you!" Dr. Doofenshmirtz yelled to his alternate self as he burst onto the balcony. "I got a little something just for you! Here!"

Everyone watched in confusion as he hurled a colorful object at Dr. Doofenshmirtz—2. But Dr. Doofenshmirtz—2 recognized it at once.

"Choo-choo?" he asked in amazement.

"Yeah, it's mine. See? I told you I never lost it," replied Dr. Doofenshmirtz. "You can have it."

"I don't believe it," Dr. Doofenshmirtz–2 murmured as he turned the old toy train over to examine it. "Choo-choo, it *is* you! Ah! Heart-melting! Backstory-resolving! Evilness-diminishing!"

"Eh, it's the least I can do," Dr. Doofenshmirtz said with a shrug. "I wish someone would come up to me and hand me something that would resolve all of *my* tragic backstories. Hint-hint. Anyone?"

"You know, I don't know what I was thinking with the whole evil-robot thing," Dr. Doofenshmirtz–2 said. "Looking around, I'm really embarrassed. Here, let me clean this up. Look. Self-destruct button!"

"Aw, you're going to be all right," Dr. Doofenshmirtz told his alternate self.

"Yeah, here we go!" Dr. Doofenshmirtz–2 said excitedly as he pressed a button on the control panel.

All over Danville, his robot army began to self-destruct and disappear—at the very moment Candace finally dragged her mom out of the movie theater.

"Mom, come on, hurry, hurry!" Candace cried as

they burst out of the theater to see . . . absolutely nothing.

"Do I even need to say there's nothing there anymore?" her mom said with a sigh.

A huge grin spread across Candace's face. For once, she was overjoyed that her mom had totally missed Phineas and Ferb's latest shenanigans!

"Mom, you can say it all you want! There's nothing there!" Candace cheered. "Woo-hoo! I did it! I saved the world! You can go back to your movie now."

Mrs. Flynn-Fletcher shook her head as she walked back into the theater. As soon as her mom was out of earshot, Candace let out a sigh of relief. What a day!

On the balcony of Doofenshmirtz Evil, Incorporated, Dr. Doofenshmirtz got ready to say good-bye to his alternate self. He stuck out his hand for a farewell handshake.

"You know, we're totally cool now," Dr. Doofenshmirtz-2 said in a friendly voice. "I'm just going to return to my home and live out my days with my choo-choo. Okay then, *ciao!*"

With one last wave, Dr. Doofenshmirtz–2 stepped through the portal to his own dimension. "Ah, home!" he said with a satisfied sigh. "It's good to be—"

His voice trailed off as he realized that an unpleasant surprise was waiting for him

"Book him, ladies," Major Monogram–2 ordered the Firestorm Girls. Candace–2's top fighters rushed forward with handcuffs.

"Heh-heh, that's right. . . . You know, my crimes against humanity just completely slipped my mind," Dr. Doofenshmirtz–2 chuckled awkwardly.

As the Firestorm Girls led away the evil scientist, Phineas–2, Ferb–2, and Candace–2 stepped through the portal to join them. At that moment, Candace arrived, too.

"Hey, did you guys just see that?" Candace exclaimed. "I saved Danville! Who knew having Mom see *nothing* could be so satisfying!"

"Good job, soldier," Candace–2 said, saluting.

"So, what will you do now?" asked Candace.

"Wow, I haven't thought of anything but busting Doofenshmirtz for years," Candace-2 replied. "I don't know."

"Well . . . I know what interests *I'd* pursue," Candace told her alternate self, nodding toward Jeremy-2 on the other side of the portal.

"Hey, here you all are," Jeremy-2 said as he stepped through the portal.

"I'll take that under consideration," Candace-2 said. She looked at her alternate self and winked. "What about you?"

"You know, after all of this, I'm going to give myself a little more time to be young," Candace said firmly. "It's not such a bad place to be."

"You know what? Me, too," Candace-2 said.

At the portal back to his own dimension, Phineas-2 paused. "Hey, I just wanted to say thanks for telling us all about summer, and, you know, opening our horizons. And teaching Ferb classical guitar."

Ferb-2 pulled out the instrument and played a

beautiful riff. Suddenly, there was a rustling in one of the piles of busted-up robots. To everyone's horror, the platyborg rose up from the debris!

Then it dropped to all fours and let out an adorable little mechanical purr.

"Hey, it's *our* Perry!" Phineas–2 exclaimed. "Looks like the evil was fried right out of him."

"Sorry he's mostly made of metal," Phineas said.

"Are you kidding?" asked Phineas–2. "That makes him *extra* cool! Thanks so much, guys!"

"I'm glad we could help," Phineas said with a wave as the alternate group climbed through the portal to their own dimension.

Then he turned to his own brother and platypus. "Man, this has been the greatest day ever," Phineas said. "Imagine how much fun we can have together now that we know you're a secret agent!"

"Yes, yes, the next fifteen minutes should be a real hoot," Major Monogram said as he and Carl arrived on the balcony. "Then, of course, Agent P will be sent away forever."

"*What?*" Phineas gasped.

"Wait, you didn't know?" Major Monogram asked. "Didn't he give you a pamphlet?"

"We threw it away," Phineas replied.

"Does *anyone* read those things?" Major Monogram said with a sigh.

"I tried to warn you, sir," Carl spoke up.

"Kids, I'm sorry, but now that Agent P's cover has been blown, you won't be allowed to see him anymore," Major Monogram told them.

Phineas's mouth dropped open as he realized something. "*That's* why you didn't want us to know your secret!" he said to Agent P. Then he turned back to Major Monogram. "So we'll never see Perry again? There *has* to be another way!"

Major Monogram shook his head. "I'm sorry, Phineas. You know too much. It isn't safe."

"I never wished so much that I could *unknow* something," Phineas said sadly.

"Sir?" Carl asked. "Maybe there *is* a way. What about Dr. Doofenshmirtz's Amnesia-inator?"

"I never built an Amnesia-inator!" Dr. Doofenshmirtz argued. "I think I'd remember building something like that."

Major Monogram ignored him. "Well, that might work. But you'd all have to agree," he said.

"So our choice is either to forget the best day ever, forget the biggest adventure we've ever had, and forget meeting Agent P—or remember today, but never see Perry again?" Phineas asked.

"Well, we've had a lot of great days, but we only have one Perry," Ferb told him.

"Agreed," Phineas replied.

"All right, everybody!" Major Monogram said. "Tall kids in the back! We just need to do a little more programming, and then we'll be ready to roll!"

As Major Monogram and Carl started to program the Amnesia-inator, Phineas and Ferb leaned down to Agent P. "Hey buddy," Phineas began. "Ferb and I just wanted to say our good-byes. You know, we thought we had finally met the real you when we found out that you were Agent P. But the fact is, pet, secret agent, they're both the real you. You are now and always have been a great pet . . . and a great friend. We're going to miss you, Agent P. I love you, pal."

"Sir?" Carl asked Major Monogram. "Are you crying?"

"No, I'm sweating through my eyes!" barked Major Monogram as he searched his pockets for a handkerchief.

"Okay, sir," Phineas called out. "We're ready!"

"Okay, Carl, we're set," Major Monogram commanded.

Carl pressed a button, and a blinding flash of light filled the balcony. A few seconds later, the kids stood there, blinking in confusion.

As Agent P, who was now back in pet mode as Perry the Platypus, scurried away and another bright light flashed, Phineas looked at Ferb and shrugged. He didn't know exactly what had just happened. But he could tell it was another awesome day of summer vacation. And with his brother and his platypus by his side, Phineas knew that they would find a spectacular way to spend it!

EXPERIENCE A NEW DIMENSION OF ADVENTURE!

DISNEY Phineas and FERB THE MOVIE

ACROSS THE 2nd DIMENSION

COMING TO DVD WITH DIGITAL COPY AUGUST 23